PENROD'S PANTS

Mary Blount Christian

Pictures by Jane Dyer

Ready-to-Read

Macmillan Publishing Company
New York

Collier Macmillan Publishers
London

To Dorothy Van Woerkom,
who will understand
–M.B.C.

To Julie,
who likes to read
–J.D.

Macmillan Publishing Company
866 Third Avenue, New York, N.Y. 10022
Collier Macmillan Canada, Inc.

Printed and bound by South China Printing Company, Hong Kong
First American Edition
10 9 8 7 6 5 4 3 2 1

The text of this book is set in 18 pt. Century Expanded.
The illustrations are rendered in pencil and watercolor.

Library of Congress Cataloging in Publication Data
Christian, Mary Blount.
Penrod's pants.
Summary: Despite Penrod Porcupine's sometimes
exasperating behavior, he and Griswold Bear
remain good friends.
[1. Porcupines–Fiction. 2. Bears–Fiction.
3. Friendships–Fiction] I. Dyer, Jane, ill. II. Title.
PZ7.C4528Pe 1986 [E] 85-11545
ISBN 0-02-718520-6

Contents

PENROD'S PANTS

Someone knocked
on the door.
It was Hyatt Giraffe.
"A package for you,"
he told Penrod Porcupine.
It was a pair of pants
from Grandmother Quill.
They were blue.
They had four pockets.
In one pocket
there was a five-dollar bill.

"I love these pants,"
  Penrod said to his friend
  Griswold Bear.
"Let's go shopping
  for another pair
  just like them."

Penrod and Griswold
went to town.

At the first store
they saw striped pants.
They saw plaid pants.
They saw pants with flowers.

"Hurry up,"
Griswold said.
"My feet hurt.
Buy some pants, any pants."

"But I want pants
just like the pants
from Grandmother Quill,"
Penrod said.

At the second store

they saw more pants.

Penrod tried on black pants.

He tried on white pants.

He tried on orange pants, too.

"My feet hurt,

and I'm tired," Griswold said.

"Buy the orange pants with pockets."

"I want pants

just like the pants

from Grandmother Quill,"

Penrod said.

9

At the third store
they saw piles of pants.
Penrod tried on short pants.
He tried on long pants.
He tried on pants with bibs.

"My feet hurt.
I'm tired.
And I'm hungry," Griswold said.
"Don't you like any
of these pants?"

"I want pants
just like the pants
from Grandmother Quill,"
Penrod said.

At the last store
Griswold said, "Look!
These pants are blue.
They have pockets.
They are just like the pants
from Grandmother Quill!"

"No," Penrod said.

"They are not like the pants
from Grandmother Quill."
He turned the pockets
inside out.

"See?" Penrod said.

"These pockets are empty.
The pants
from Grandmother Quill
had a five-dollar bill
in the pocket."

JUST PERFECT

Griswold had bought a pair of pants.

He put them on.

He turned around and around.

"Those pants are just perfect,"
Penrod said.
"Almost."

"What do you mean, almost?"
Griswold asked.

"They are a bit long,"
Penrod said.
"But do not worry.
I will fix them.
Take them off."

17

Snip! Snip! Snip!

Penrod cut the pants.

Griswold put on the pants.

"They are just perfect now,"
Penrod said.

"Almost."

"*Grrrrr!*" Griswold said.
"What is wrong with them?"

"Oh, nothing," Penrod said.
"But your left leg is shorter
than your right leg."

"*Grrrrr!*" Griswold said.
"My legs are exactly
   the same length."

"Ummmm," Penrod said.
"Then the left pant leg is longer
   than the right pant leg.
   Do not worry.
   I will fix it."

Snip! Snip! Snip!

Penrod cut the left pant leg.

Griswold put on the pants again.

"Ummmm," Penrod said.

"Now the right pant leg is longer
than the left pant leg."

Snip! Snip! Snip!

Penrod cut some more.

Griswold put on his pants.

"*Grrrrr!*" he said.

"Now both pant legs are the same.

But they are too short for me!"

"But they are just perfect
for me!" Penrod said.

THE TEA PARTY

That afternoon
Griswold had a tea party.
He invited Penrod.
They ate and ate.
At last one cookie was left
on the plate.
Penrod took it.

"Penrod!" Griswold said.
"It is not polite
to take the last cookie."

"Why not?" Penrod asked.
"You did not want it."

"How do you know that?"
Griswold said.
"Did you ask me?"

Penrod shrugged.
"If you had wanted the cookie,
you would have taken it first."

Griswold shook his head.

"It is not polite

to take the last cookie.

I will show you."

He went to the kitchen.

He got one more cookie.

"Watch me," he said.

He passed the cookie to Penrod.

"Would you like this cookie?"

he asked.

"Yes, thank you," Penrod said.

He took the cookie.

"*Grrrrr!*" Griswold said.

"Now what did I do?"
Penrod asked.

"You took the last cookie!"
Griswold said.

"But you asked me!"
Penrod said.

"I was showing you
how to be polite!"
Griswold said.

Penrod munched the cookie.
"I was polite," he said.
"I waited until you asked me.
And I said thank you."

"*Grrrrr!*" Griswold said.
He got one more cookie
from the kitchen.
"Let's try it again.
This time you offer the cookie
to me."

"Would you like this cookie?"
Penrod asked.

Griswold patted his mouth
with his napkin.
"Oh, no, thank you.
I could not eat another bite."

"Good!" Penrod said.
He popped the cookie
into his mouth.

"*Grrrrr!*" Griswold said.
"You did it all wrong again!"

"But you said
    you did not want it,"
    Penrod said.

"I was being polite,"
    Griswold said.
"Let us try it one more time."

He got the very last cookie
from the kitchen.
"Now," Griswold said,
"I will offer you the cookie.
You will say 'no, thank you'
even if you want the cookie.
Understand?"

Penrod shook his head.
"What will happen to the cookie?"

Griswold smiled.
"We can break it in half
and each take a piece," he said.

"That way neither of us
  will get enough cookie,"
Penrod said.

"Or we could leave it
  on the plate," Griswold said.

"Then neither of us
  will get *any* cookie!"
Penrod said.

"But we will both be polite,"
Griswold said.

"I will take the plate
  back to the kitchen,"
Penrod said.

"Why, thank you,"
Griswold said.
"That is very polite!"

"Thank *you*,"
Penrod said.
And he popped the last cookie
into his mouth.

SCARY NIGHT

Later Penrod and Griswold

walked to the park.

They played on the swings.

They played on the slide.

They played on the seesaw.

They played until dark.

"I am afraid
   to walk home alone,"
   Penrod said.

"Do not be afraid,"
   Griswold said.
"I will walk home
   with you."

Griswold walked home
   with Penrod.
"Now *I* am afraid
   to walk home alone,"
   Griswold said.

"You can spend the night
with me,"
Penrod said.
"You can sleep on the couch."

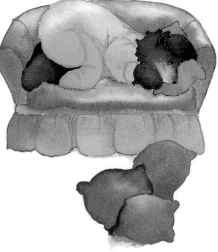

Griswold tossed.

Griswold turned.

He flipped and he flopped.

He woke up Penrod.

"It is no use," he said.

"I cannot sleep

without my blanket."

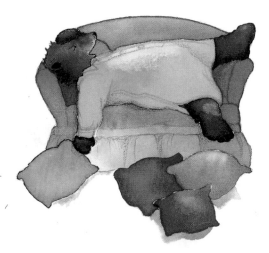

Penrod walked Griswold
to his house.
"Now *I* am afraid
to walk home alone,"
Penrod said.

"You can sleep on *my* couch,"
Griswold said.

Penrod tossed.

Penrod turned.

Penrod flipped and flopped.

He woke up Griswold.

"It is no use," he said.

"I cannot sleep
without my pillow."

Griswold walked Penrod home.
But Griswold was afraid
to walk home alone.
So Penrod walked him home again.

"I am tired,"
Griswold said.
"I cannot do this all night."

Penrod looked at the sky.
It was getting light.
"We already did this all night,"
he said.
"Now I am not afraid
to go home alone."

Penrod waved good-bye.
He walked through the gate
straight to his house
next door.

THE TOOTH

"Oh, oh!" Griswold said
  the next day.
"My tooth is loose!"

"Pull it out," Penrod said.

"I am afraid."

"Do not worry," Penrod said.
"I will help you."

Penrod gave Griswold an apple.

"Chew this," he said.

"Ooooooh!" Griswold said.

But the tooth did not come out.

Penrod tied a string
to Griswold's tooth.
He tied the other end
of the string
to the doorknob.
"Get down on your knees,"
Penrod said.
"When I close the door
it will pull out your tooth.
One. Two."

"Stop!" Griswold said.
"Do not count out loud.
Surprise me."

Penrod counted to himself.
One. Two. Three.
He slammed the door shut.

"Owwww!" Griswold said.
The doorknob had come off.
It had hit his nose.
"Now I have a loose tooth
and a sore nose!"

49

"Do not worry," Penrod said.

"I have another plan."

He led Griswold to a tree.

"Climb up the tree,"

Penrod said.

"Tie this string to the branch.

Then jump!"

Griswold moaned.

"I cannot do that.

It has to be a surprise.

You will have to push me,"

he said.

"No!" Penrod said.
"You know I am afraid
to climb trees."

"I will help you,"
Griswold said.
Penrod closed his eyes
while Griswold helped him up.
"I have to close my eyes now,"
Griswold said.
"You will have to open yours."

51

Penrod opened his eyes.

He looked down.

The ground looked far away.

"Oh, oh!" he said.

He shook with fear.

"Stop shaking!" Griswold said.

"The branch will break."

Snap! The branch broke.

Down went Griswold.

Bump went the branch
on Griswold's head.

Thump went Penrod
beside him.

"Ooooooh!" Griswold said.
"Now you have done it!
My feet hurt
from shopping for pants
with you.
You gave me a sore nose.
You gave me a bump
on the head."

"But look!" Penrod said.
"There is your tooth!
It is on the ground,
not in your mouth!"

Griswold picked up his tooth.

"So it is," he said.

"And I really was surprised."

Griswold yawned.

He turned and walked away.

"Where are you going?"

Penrod asked.

"I am going to put this tooth
under my pillow.
Then I am going to sleep.
And, if you are lucky, Penrod,
by spring I may think
this was funny."

"Sleep tight!" Penrod called.
"When you wake up,
we will have even *more* fun."

"*Grrrrr!*" Griswold said.